Knights Don't
Teach Piano

There are more books about the Bailey School Kids!
Have you read these adventures?

Knights Don't Teach Piano

by Debbie Dadey
and
Marcia Thornton Jones

illustrated by John Steven Gurney

A
LITTLE APPLE
PAPERBACK

SCHOLASTIC INC.
New York   Toronto   London   Auckland   Sydney

ISBN 0-590-25804-4

Text copyright © 1998 by Marcia Thornton Jones and Debra S. Dadey.
Illustrations copyright © 1998 by Scholastic Inc.
All rights reserved. Published by Scholastic Inc.
LITTLE APPLE PAPERBACKS is a trademark of Scholastic Inc.
THE ADVENTURES OF THE BAILEY SCHOOL KIDS in design is a registered trademark of Scholastic Inc.

12 11 10 9 8 7 6 5 4 3 2   8 9/9 0 1/0 2/0

Printed in the U.S.A.   40

First Scholastic printing, January 1998

Book design by Laurie Williams

Contents

1

Party Time

"Happy birthday to you," Melody sang to Eddie. "You look like a monkey and you smell like one, too!"

"Very funny, monkey breath," Eddie said, tugging on one of Melody's black pigtails. "You should be glad this is my birthday or I wouldn't be in such a good mood."

"This is a great party," Liza said from behind Melody.

Howie looked around Eddie's basement and nodded. Balloons, streamers, and happy birthday banners hung from the ceiling. A huge birthday cake with nine candles, cups filled with juice, and party favors covered one table. "Your grandmother thought of everything," Howie told Eddie.

"I really like the knight theme," Liza said. "Your grandmother found lots of cool stuff about castles and knights. She even found tiny shields for everybody."

"That's so I can protect myself from you," Eddie said, holding his shield in front of her face. "And my grandmother said she still has one big surprise left for me."

Melody looked at the pile of opened presents and put her hands on her hips. "I can't believe you're going to get another present. You already have all this neat stuff."

Eddie smiled. "I guess I'm lucky, in addition to being good-looking."

Melody bopped Eddie on the head with her knight shield. "If you're good-looking, then I'm King Kong."

"Ouch," Eddie complained, running his hand through his red hair. "Why don't you go climb the Empire State Building and leave my head alone?"

"Oh, my gosh," Liza squealed as she looked behind Eddie.

"What's wrong?" Eddie said. "Did she make me bleed?"

Liza shook her head. "You're not going to believe what's behind you."

Eddie's grandmother put her hands over Eddie's eyes. "Eddie," she said, "your surprise is here."

"All right," Eddie said. "Can I see it?"

Melody, Liza, and Howie stared behind Eddie. As a matter of fact, everyone at

the party couldn't take their eyes off Eddie's surprise.

"This is so cool," Howie told Eddie.

Eddie jumped up and down. "Let me see!"

Liza patted Eddie on the shoulder. "You should thank your grandmother for this," Liza said.

"Thanks, Grandma," Eddie said. "It was nice of you to give me this party and the surprise."

"It is sooooooo neat," Melody said.

"Can I see it?" Eddie shrieked.

Eddie's grandmother took her hands off Eddie's eyes and spun him around.

2

Birthday Surprise

Eddie twirled around and came face-to-face with a silver monster. "Aaaahh!" Eddie yelled and fell back against his grandmother.

Eddie's grandmother gave Eddie a little shove. "I'd like you to meet Mr. Lance E. Lott," she said. "He's your surprise."

"Wow," Howie said.

"You are *so* lucky," Melody said.

Liza nodded. "This is the best birthday surprise in the world."

Eddie looked at the tall man in silver armor. He had a blond pointy beard and his eyes looked like two black marbles. But that's not what Eddie stared at. Lance's chest looked like it was covered with a huge pizza pan. Under the shield, he wore a suit made out of black chain

6

mesh. His arms and legs were completely covered by it. The faceplate on his silver helmet was pushed up, and a royal purple feather curled above his head. He looked exactly like the bad knight in a movie Eddie once saw, except Lance wasn't sitting on top of a black horse. Instead, the knight was standing right in front of him.

"Cool," Eddie said. "My own private knight. Just let a teacher try giving me homework now."

"Oh, no," Eddie's grandmother said with a laugh. "I mean Lance has your surprise."

"Happy birthday, Sir Edward," Lance said with a British accent. Then Lance bowed to Eddie. When he did, the faceplate slapped down over his nose with a loud clang.

Melody giggled, but Liza and Howie stared at the knight as if he had just handed Eddie a king's crown. Nobody ever called Eddie by his full name of Edward and got away with it. And no one had ever called Eddie "sir" before. Nobody wanted to.

But Eddie didn't notice. He rubbed his hands together. Whatever his surprise was, it had to be good. After all, anything a cool dude in armor brought had to be even better than fake snot.

"I bet it's a sword," Eddie said. "Is it?"

"No," his grandmother said. "Guess again."

"The shield," Eddie said hopefully, eyeing the silver shield Lance held in his hand.

Eddie's grandmother shook her head and smiled. "No," she said. "It's better than a sword or a shield. Tell him, Lance."

Eddie and his three friends stared up at the stranger dressed in armor. Lance took a step forward. When he did, the sun glinted off his chest plate and made Melody squint. Lance handed Eddie a white envelope sealed with a bloodred blob of wax. "Your gift, sir," Lance said.

Eddie tore open the envelope to read the card inside. He read it once, then reread it.

"What's wrong?" Howie asked.

"Your face is as white as vanilla ice cream," Melody said.

"Are you okay?" Liza asked.

Eddie didn't answer. Instead, he held up the card for his friends to read.

3

Eddie's Fault

"It's all your fault," Melody told Eddie, squinting her eyes in the meanest look she could. It was the day after Eddie's party. The four friends had met in their favorite meeting place, under the oak tree on the school playground.

Eddie stomped his foot in a puddle of slush. "Don't blame me. It was my grandmother's idea for me to take piano lessons from Lance. I had nothing to do with it."

"Yes, you did," Liza said. "As soon as my mom found out about your piano lessons, she called Lance and signed me up."

"Then she called my mom and Howie's dad," Melody added. "Now we all have to learn to play the piano."

"And it wasn't even our birthdays!" Liza groaned.

"You're making it sound much worse than it is," Howie told his friends. "My old piano teacher was fun and Mr. Lott might be even better."

"Do you mean you *like* to take piano lessons?" Melody asked.

"Well," Howie said, "it's not so bad. Besides, if we get good enough, we can play in a rock-and-roll band."

"True," Liza said. "It might be kind of neat, and Lance does seem nice."

"That's right," Howie said. "How many other grown-ups would go to all that trouble to dress up like a knight because your grandmother asked?"

"Grandmother didn't ask him to dress like that," Eddie said. "Lance did it on his own. Grandma said he must be one of those eccentric British musicians."

"Do you mean Lance E. Lott always dresses like a knight?" Melody asked.

"I guess so. Taking piano lessons from Lance wouldn't be bad if he really were a knight," Eddie admitted. "Then maybe he could teach me to sword fight, too."

"Whoever heard of a knight teaching piano?" Liza said with a giggle.

"Whoever heard of giving piano lessons for a birthday present?" Eddie grumbled.

13

But his friends didn't hear him because just then a black horse galloped across the Bailey School playground. Perched on top of the horse was Mr. Lance E. Lott.

4

Something Strange

After school on Monday afternoon, Eddie and Howie crossed Forest Lane and hiked down Green Street.

"Grandma said Lance lives right past the city limits," Eddie said.

"That explains his horse," Howie said.

"But it doesn't explain why he galloped through Bailey City," Eddie said.

"He probably got lost," Howie said.

"Maybe," Eddie said when he stopped to rest at the gate leading to Lance's house. "But if you ask me, there is something strange about a piano teacher who wears armor and races around on a gigantic black horse."

"Look at that house," Howie said.

"I've never seen a house that big before," Eddie said. The two boys couldn't help staring.

Howie nodded. "It's so big, it doesn't even look like a house. It looks more like a . . ."

"A castle," Eddie finished.

The two boys looked at the tall gray building. The corners were rounded and the top floor had turrets like a castle.

"Let's get this over with," Eddie said as they pounded on the front door.

The door creaked open and Lance smiled down at Howie and Eddie. Lance still wore the same shiny armor he had worn to Eddie's birthday party, except without the helmet. "Welcome," Lance said. He led the boys down a long dark hallway. They passed three big rooms full of dark furniture before Lance led them into the music room. Against one wall was an ancient-looking piano. On another wall hung a huge picture of a woman wearing a gold crown on her head.

"That sure is an old piano," Howie said.

Lance nodded. "I brought it with me from England," he said. "It has been in my family for generations."

"Is that your mother?" Eddie asked, pointing to the picture of the lady.

Lance bowed his head when he faced the picture. "No," he told them. "That is my queen. Now, who would like to play first?" Lance asked.

Eddie ducked his head and kicked at the carpet. He didn't say a word.

"I'll go first," Howie said.

"Wonderful," Lance said. While Lance showed Howie how to hold his fingers and play a scale, Eddie wandered down the hall and into a huge kitchen. A bowl filled with sugar cubes sat in the middle of an old wooden table. Eddie tried to build a castle out of the sugar cubes, but

they kept falling down. He ended up eating four sugar cubes before he noticed a door at the other end of the kitchen. He stuffed two more sugar cubes in his shirt pocket for later.

Eddie looked down the hall. He could still hear Howie plunking away on Lance's ancient piano. Lance and Howie hadn't even noticed he was gone.

Eddie walked to the closed door and grabbed the handle to pull it open. When he did he was surprised to find what was behind the door.

5

Phe-ew!

"Holy Toledo," Eddie gasped. He stumbled into a big hall. A huge round table stood exactly in the center of the room. The table wasn't what made Eddie gasp, though. It was what sat in the six throne-like chairs surrounding the table. Every chair but one had a suit of brightly polished armor sitting upright in it.

Slowly, Eddie inched his way to one of the suits of armor. With trembling fingers he lifted the visor on the helmet and peered inside.

"Empty," Eddie said, backing away from the table as if he expected the suits of armor to jump up and grab him. "What a weird thing for someone to have in his house. Hasn't Lance ever heard of a big-screen TV?"

Eddie turned to leave when he heard a creak. He looked at the ghostlike suits of armor. "All right," Eddie yelled. "Which one of you moved?"

None of the suits answered, so Eddie inched back over to the table and slowly, as if he were afraid it would bite, lifted another visor. Eddie ran around the table and lifted each visor. Every suit of armor was empty. Eddie even banged on a couple of chests just to be sure they were hollow.

"If you're all empty, then what made that sound?" Eddie asked the suits. The armor didn't answer, but something else did.

A noise came from behind a heavy purple velvet curtain. Eddie pushed the curtain aside and looked out the window. The door to a stone building was swinging in the breeze as if somebody had just run through it.

"Whatever you are," Eddie said, "I've got you now." Without even looking back,

Eddie jumped out the window and ran to the stone building.

Snort! Snort! Eddie heard a sound from behind the swinging door. Eddie looked around. Not a soul in sight. He could still hear the faint tinkling of piano keys from inside the house.

Snort! Eddie gulped and decided to peek inside the old building. Slowly, he pushed on the door. *Eeeek. Eeeek.* Eddie poked his head into the dark building.

He smelled hay, a musty smell, and then something that caused him to jerk his head back outside. "Phe-ew," Eddie said, gasping for fresh air. "Something smells bad." He had smelled that smell before, but he couldn't remember where.

Holding his nose, Eddie squeezed through the door. This time he slid his whole body inside. It took a few minutes for his eyes to adjust to the dark building.

Finally, he could make out shapes along one wall. They were long, pointy shapes. Some had blades at the end, but most were spearlike. Next to the spearlike things were swords. "It looks like someone is getting ready for a full-scale war," Eddie whispered.

Snort! The sound caused Eddie to jump. Slowly, Eddie turned around to face the creature that had made the sound.

"A horse!" Eddie said with relief. But it was no ordinary horse. It was the giant

black horse they'd seen Lance riding. Its legs were the size of telephone poles and its head nearly touched the ceiling of the old building. "You sure have been taking your vitamins," Eddie said with a giggle.

"*Snort*," said the horse. It took a step closer to Eddie.

"Nice horsey," Eddie said, holding up a hand. "I come in peace." Eddie stepped back until he bumped into a sword. He knocked over the sword, causing a chain reaction. Every sword fell over, and then the spears clattered down. They all crashed to the wooden floor.

"Oooops," Eddie said.

"*Snort*," said the horse, stepping still closer.

Eddie tried to edge toward the door, but the horse had him trapped. The horse reached his huge nose toward Eddie, his hot breath blowing on Eddie's face.

"Aaah," Eddie gulped. "Don't eat me."

The horse started chewing, all right. He munched and munched. It took Eddie a minute to realize the horse wasn't eating him. The horse was eating the sugar cubes out of his pocket.

When the horse finished, it snorted and walked away. Eddie took the chance to zip out the swinging door. When he was outside, he gasped, "Whew, that was a little too close for comfort." Then he smelled the terrible smell again. It was very strong this time.

"Oh, no," Eddie said as he looked down. He suddenly remembered where he had smelled that smell before. The Bailey City Stables had that same smell. It was horse manure, and Eddie was standing in a huge pile of it.

6

The Most Famous Knight of All

"I'm telling you, Lance is planning a war on Bailey City," Eddie told his friends. It was after the boys' piano lessons and the kids were gathered under the oak tree.

Liza shook her head. "Just because you hate taking piano lessons doesn't mean you should talk badly about your teacher," she told Eddie.

"I don't hate the lessons," Eddie explained. "As a matter of fact, they were kind of fun. But that has nothing to do with the fact that Lance is planning to take over our town."

Howie put his hand on Eddie's shoulder. "I think that horse manure caused you to get a little light-headed."

Melody giggled. "Why would a piano teacher declare war on Bailey City?"

"You're forgetting that Lance isn't an ordinary piano teacher," Eddie explained. "He's a knight in shining armor. He's probably the leader of a whole group of knights. That's why he has those suits of armor. He and his friends are plotting to overthrow the mayor."

Liza rolled her eyes. "I think you've flipped out," she told Eddie. "You're wacko."

"You won't think I'm nuts when Lance turns you into a court jester," Eddie said.

"Mr. Lance E. Lott is a perfectly nice man," Liza said, pointing her finger at Eddie. "You owe him an apology for saying mean things about him."

"What did you say?" Eddie asked.

Liza put her hands on her hips. "I said you should tell Lance you're sorry."

"No," Eddie said, smacking himself in the forehead. "Why didn't I catch it before?"

"Catch what," Melody giggled, "the measles?"

"No," Eddie said. "Don't you get it?"

Eddie stared at the blank faces of his three friends. "Lance's name," Eddie said, "is Lance E. Lott. That stands for the most famous knight of all."

"You mean —" Howie said.

"That's right," Eddie interrupted, "Lance is really Lancelot. And he's here to make Bailey City his new kingdom."

7

Eddie's Plan

Howie, Melody, and Liza stared at Eddie for a full minute. It was completely quiet except for the cold wind rattling the empty branches over their heads.

"But Lancelot was a knight of the round table," Howie finally said.

Eddie nodded. "Now you're getting it."

"The only thing we're getting," Melody said, "is mad at you for being so silly."

"But I saw the round table," Eddie yelled. "Complete with armor, ready and waiting for the next meeting of knights."

"And I saw Hercules dancing with your grandmother," Melody said with a laugh.

Eddie thumped Melody on the arm. "The only difference between your Hercules and my knight is that Lancelot is real."

"Well," Howie said, "he *was* real."

"But that was hundreds of years ago," Liza added. "When Lancelot was a knight in King Arthur's Camelot."

"This is today in Bailey City. Not Camelot," Melody said with her hands on her hips.

"Besides," Liza said with a giggle, "I'm pretty sure knights didn't play 'Chopsticks' in Camelot."

"And they definitely don't teach piano in Bailey City," added Melody.

Howie smiled. "Liza and Melody are right. Knights had sword fights and rode big horses."

"Giant horses," Eddie said slowly. "Just like the one that tried to eat me when I was in Lance's barn."

"It was eating the sugar in your pocket," Melody reminded him. "You'd be too sour for him to eat."

"Very funny, lemon-head," Eddie snapped. "But you won't be laughing when Lance and his knightly friends thunder into Bailey City!"

Melody and Howie smiled, but Liza laughed out loud. "Even if Lance were the famous knight," Liza told Eddie, "it wouldn't be so bad. After all, Lancelot and the rest of King Arthur's knights did good deeds."

"Lancelot did do good deeds," Howie said slowly. "Until he decided he wanted to rule Camelot himself."

"Exactly," Eddie said. "He fought King Arthur for Camelot, but he lost."

"See," Melody said. "You're admitting that Lancelot is dead."

Howie grabbed Melody's arm. "A normal knight would have died," Howie told Melody. "But we're forgetting one thing. Camelot had a wizard. The wizard had special magic that kept King Arthur alive."

"And he could keep Lancelot alive, too," Eddie said as if he'd just solved

fifty math problems. "Lancelot couldn't get Camelot, so he's after something else."

"What?" Liza asked.

Eddie looked each of his friends in the eyes before answering. "Lance is after Bailey City," he finally said. "And it's up to us to stop him!"

8

Crazy

"I think Eddie got something he didn't expect for his birthday," Melody told Liza the next afternoon.

"What?" Liza asked.

"He got crazy!" Melody said.

Melody and Liza skipped down Green Street, laughing. A few lazy snowflakes floated down from the sky, and Liza tried to catch one on her tongue. It was time for their first piano lesson. They were both excited, but they couldn't forget what Eddie told them the day before.

"Eddie's not crazy," Liza said. "He just got carried away with that knight theme from his birthday party."

"Maybe you're right," Melody said. "But he's still crazy."

Melody and Liza were both laughing

about Eddie when they came to the mail-box that said Lance E. Lott. They stared at the huge house until the January wind made their teeth chatter.

"Well," Liza said with a shiver, "Eddie was right about one thing."

Melody nodded. "Lance's house definitely looks like a castle," she said.

"Come on," Liza said. "If we don't hurry inside, our fingers will freeze and we won't be able to play the piano."

Melody and Liza ran up the long drive-way and reached for the door knocker. Lance swung open the door and smiled down at them. His armor glowed in the afternoon light.

"Please, do enter," he said. "I am ready to begin. We will have to hurry."

"Why?" Melody asked.

"I — I have a . . . meeting," Lance stammered, "right after your lesson. So please, let us begin." Lance led both girls down the hall and into the music room.

Liza scooted over a pile of folders and perched on a nearby couch to watch Melody.

Lance smiled at Liza. "There's hot chocolate in the kitchen. Help yourself while Melody has her lesson."

Liza thanked Mr. Lott, but shook her head. "Maybe I should watch so I'll know what to do when it's my turn."

Melody followed Mr. Lott's directions, and soon her fingers were going up and down the keys. He even showed her how to play a tune using all the fingers on her right hand.

When it was Liza's turn, Melody scooped up her music folder so Liza could sit on the ancient piano stool. Liza curved her fingers just like Melody had. But when Liza tried to hit a key with one finger, she ended up hitting two keys. Then her fingers slipped and she banged a black key. Her playing didn't sound like Melody's at all.

Lance didn't look worried. He sat up straight, smiled, and showed her the right way.

Melody sat on the cluttered couch for a while, but when she started squirming Mr. Lott suggested she get some hot chocolate. Melody grabbed her music folder and trotted toward the kitchen.

The kitchen was at the end of the hall. Melody sat at the kitchen table sipping warm cocoa and listening to Liza's piano playing. Every time Liza hit a wrong note, Melody cringed. Melody cringed a lot. Liza's plunking was getting on Melody's nerves.

Melody looked around and saw the heavy door at the end of the kitchen. Maybe she wouldn't be able to hear Liza's bad notes from behind that door.

Melody pulled open the door and stared at the round table Eddie had de-scribed. Melody laid her music folder on the ancient table. The wood was scarred with deep scratches. She slowly walked

around the table and examined each suit of armor. Mr. Lott obviously liked collecting armor.

She was ready to go back to the music room when she accidentally knocked her music to the floor. Papers scattered everywhere. Melody crawled around, gathering her loose papers. That's when she saw it.

9

Worrywarts

"Where have you been?" Liza asked Melody. "I looked all around Mr. Lott's house for you and it's freezing out here." The two girls stood outside the castlelike house after their lessons.

Melody put her hand on Liza's shoulder. "I found something weird mixed in with my music. I think Eddie was right about Lance really being Lancelot," Melody said.

"If Eddie was right, then it must be the end of the world," Liza said.

Melody was serious. "I saw a map of Bailey City Park. It looked like a battle plan," she said.

"Let me see the map," Liza asked, pulling her coat tight around her.

"I put it back on the couch," Melody

told Liza. "I didn't want Lance to know I'd seen it."

Liza and Melody trudged toward home. By the time they walked by the playground, Melody had convinced Liza that Lance was ready to take over Bailey City. They ran up to Howie and Eddie. The boys were under the big oak tree trying to drive Howie's remote control car up the side of the tree.

"I'm worried," Liza told the boys.

Eddie rolled his eyes. "You're always worried about something. You are the Queen of the Worrywarts."

"But this is serious," Melody said. "I found something terrible in Lance's house."

"Cool," Eddie said. "What was it?"

"A map," Melody told him. And then she explained about the mysterious map and its battle plans.

"If you were right about Lance being Lancelot," Howie said, holding his car in

one hand and his remote control in the other, "we might be in danger."

"I think we should do something," Liza said.

"Let's go," Eddie said. "I'll show you the weapons in his barn. Maybe we'll find a clue there." There was nothing Eddie liked better than snooping. Howie tucked his remote control car under one arm and stuffed the controller into his jeans pocket. The four kids took off toward Lance's house.

They darted from one tree to the next as they made their way up the long lane in front of Lance's house.

"I think we're being silly," Howie told his friends. "Let's go back and play with my remote control car."

"Shhh," Melody said. "Someone is coming." The kids hid behind a big maple tree just as six giant horses thundered out of Lance E. Lott's stable. On each horse was a knight in shining armor carrying a long spearlike stick.

The kids froze just as a loud voice said, "We'll destroy them!"

10

Jousting

"The time has come," Lance said in a booming voice. The kids peeked from behind the tree. Lance pointed to one of the men, who had a blue ribbon tied around his arm. "Tomorrow, we ride into Bailey City Park and take Bailey City," Lance said and held up a wrinkled paper.

Melody grabbed Liza's arm. "It's the map," Melody whispered.

"I have planned our every move on this map," Lance told the other knights.

The knight wearing the blue ribbon urged his white horse one step closer to Lance. "We're tired of your plans," the knight said.

"The time to act is *now!*" another knight said.

"Bailey City is my city," the man with

the blue ribbon cried and held his weapon high in the air. "I will defend her until the end."

"Then I will have to stop you and whoever stands with you," Lance said.

The knight with the blue ribbon placed his hand over his heart. "I am Simon of Bailey City. I stand for justice. Whoever stands with me will wear my colors." Two men rode their horses next to Simon and tied blue ribbons around their arms.

"Let the battle begin," Lance shouted.

The men quickly lined their horses up. Lance and two knights faced the three blue-ribbon knights. Their horses thundered forward until they were so close the knights could whack each other with their weapons.

"What are they doing?" Liza whispered.

"It's called jousting," Howie whispered back.

Eddie gulped. "I think it's called trying to kill each other."

Whack. Slam. Whack. Slam. The men battled dangerously close to the kids' hiding place. Liza closed her eyes and grabbed Melody's arm.

"If they find us," Melody whispered, "we're dead."

Eddie motioned for everyone to run. Liza started to run, but Howie was too busy watching the knights joust.

"*Ooomph.*" Liza tripped into Howie and knocked him down. Howie sat right on the remote control of his race car.

Simon pulled to a stop so suddenly his horse reared up. "What is this?" Simon demanded as Howie's car raced straight onto the battlefield.

11

A Spy in Our Midst

Simon jumped off his horse and held up the shiny remote control car for the other knights to see. "We have a spy in our midst," Simon roared.

Lance peered around the big tree. There stood Melody, Liza, Eddie, and Howie.

Eddie gasped. "I told you we should have run."

"What are you doing here?" Lance demanded.

"We aren't spies," Liza whimpered. "We're piano players."

"But we're not going to let you take over Bailey City," Melody said boldly. She stood up tall to prove how brave she was.

Lance laughed so hard his armor rat-

tled. "And what makes you think we plan to take over the city?" he asked.

Liza cleared her throat. "Excuse me, sir," she said. "But you are wearing armor."

"After all, piano teachers don't invite friends over for sword fights," Howie added.

"And they don't keep a map of Bailey City," Melody said, "with red battle plans drawn on it."

"The map?" Lance growled. "You saw the map?"

Melody nodded. "We know what you're planning, but we won't let you invade Bailey City!"

"Do you really think you can stop the knights of the round table?" Lance asked.

Two of the knights drew their daggers. Simon dropped Howie's car and hopped back on his horse. The six knights faced Eddie, Liza, Melody, and Howie, towering above them on their snorting steeds.

"We'd like to see you stop us," Simon

said with a grin. "May we ask how you plan to do it?"

"Tell them, Eddie," Melody said.

"Why me?" Eddie asked. "I think Howie should tell them. He's the smart one."

Howie choked and pointed at Liza. "Liza, you tell them," he said.

Liza just stared at the six knights.

"They can't stop us," Lance said. "No one can stop us!"

Eddie pushed past Howie. "Is that a dare?" he sputtered.

"A double dare," Lance said, leaning forward in his saddle.

"You'll be sorry you ever said that," Eddie said. "Because I have a sweet surprise for you." Eddie reached deep into his shirt pocket. He pulled out a tiny white cube.

Snort. Lance's horse perked its ears toward the sugar cube. Eddie pulled out more sugar cubes and stacked them on the ground.

Snort. Snort. Three more horses looked at Eddie. When Eddie reached into his pocket for more sugar, all the horses started moving toward him.

Simon pulled back on his reins, but his horse ignored him and headed for the pile of sugar cubes. Lance's horse tried to step in front of Simon's horse.

Lance pulled and tugged to stop his horse. When he did, the map of Bailey City fluttered in the wind and blew away. Lance didn't notice. He was too busy trying to stop his horse from galloping to the sugar cubes.

"RUN!" Howie yelled as he dashed down the lane. Liza and Eddie were close on his heels, but Melody veered to the right and grabbed the map from the ground.

And then Melody raced after her friends.

12

Another Surprise

"Where are you taking us?" Eddie asked. It was Saturday morning, several days after the four kids fled Lance's house. Eddie's grandmother was leading the four friends down Main Street toward a special surprise.

"If I tell you, it would ruin the surprise," his grandmother said. "But if you don't hurry, we'll miss it."

As they got closer to Bailey City Park, they passed more and more people. They were all heading in the same direction.

"What's going on?" Howie asked. "Is it a parade?"

"Maybe it's a carnival," Liza said.

Eddie's grandmother shook her head. "It's even better," she said, pointing to a huge banner hanging between two trees. The banner said:

Medieval Festival

"Wow," Melody said when she saw a horse and rider gallop by.

"The Bailey City Seniors Club planned this event. Isn't it wonderful?" Eddie's grandmother said. "Now let's hurry so we can get a good seat for the jousting match."

"The jousting match?" Melody shouted.

"Well, of course," Eddie's grandmother said. "What fun would a Medieval Festival be without knights in shining armor having a fight?"

The four friends and Eddie's grandmother climbed to the top of the bleachers just as five knights on huge horses rode into the park. They circled the park once and then dismounted, ready to fight each other. A lady in a long velvet dress

pretended she needed help. Eddie's grandmother clapped and cheered along with the crowd.

Melody wasn't cheering. "Did you notice something's missing?" she asked.

Howie, Eddie, and Liza looked around the park. They shook their heads.

"Try counting the knights," she said. "Lance is missing."

"Of course he is," Eddie's grandmother said. "He phoned me last night. He had to rush back to England. He was sorry he couldn't continue your piano lessons."

Eddie started to cheer, but he didn't want to hurt his grandmother's feelings.

"It's too bad about your birthday present," Eddie's grandmother said. "I'll get you something else."

"A video game would be fine with me," Eddie suggested.

"Oh, posh, video games aren't creative. How about a flute?" his grandmother asked. Then she cheered for the knights again.

Eddie groaned. Howie and Melody giggled at the thought of Eddie playing a flute.

Liza sighed. "I think playing a flute would be nice."

"As long as the flute teacher doesn't have a sword hidden somewhere," Howie joked.

"Lance wasn't really a knight," Eddie said. "None of them were. They were just actors getting ready for this festival."

"I guess it was silly to believe Lance was the famous Lancelot," Liza said. "After all, knights don't teach piano."

"Maybe," Melody said. She patted her pocket where she had hidden Lance's map. "But I'll hang onto this map . . . just to be sure."

Debbie Dadey and Marcia Thornton Jones have fun writing stories together. When they both worked at an elementary school in Lexington, Kentucky, Debbie was the school librarian and Marcia was a teacher. During their lunch break in the school cafeteria, they came up with the idea of the Bailey School kids.

Recently Debbie and her family moved to Aurora, Illinois. Marcia and her husband still live in Kentucky where she continues to teach. How do these authors still write together? They talk on the phone and use computers and fax machines!

Creepy, weird, wacky and funny things happen to the Bailey School Kids!™ Collect and read them all!

The Adventures of THE BAILEY SCHOOL KIDS ®

☐ BAS43411-X	#1	Vampires Don't Wear Polka Dots	$2.99	✓
☐ BAS44061-6	#2	Werewolves Don't Go to Summer Camp	$2.99	
☐ BAS44477-8	#3	Santa Claus Doesn't Mop Floors	$2.99	
☐ BAS44822-6	#4	Leprechauns Don't Play Basketball	$2.99	✓
☐ BAS45854-X	#5	Ghosts Don't Eat Potato Chips	$2.99	✓
☐ BAS47071-X	#6	Frankenstein Doesn't Plant Petunias	$2.99	✓
☐ BAS47070-1	#7	Aliens Don't Wear Braces	$2.99	✓
☐ BAS47297-6	#8	Genies Don't Ride Bicycles	$2.99	✓
☐ BAS47298-4	#9	Pirates Don't Wear Pink Sunglasses	$2.99	✓
☐ BAS48112-6	#10	Witches Don't Do Backflips	$2.99	✓
☐ BAS48113-4	#11	Skeletons Don't Play Tubas	$2.99	✓
☐ BAS48114-2	#12	Cupid Doesn't Flip Hamburgers	$2.99	
☐ BAS48115-0	#13	Gremlins Don't Chew Bubble Gum	$2.99	
☐ BAS22635-5	#14	Monsters Don't Scuba Dive	$2.99	
☐ BAS22636-3	#15	Zombies Don't Play Soccer	$2.99	
☐ BAS22638-X	#16	Dracula Doesn't Drink Lemonade	$2.99	✓
☐ BAS22637-1	#17	Elves Don't Wear Hard Hats	$2.99	
☐ BAS50960-8	#18	Martians Don't Take Temperatures	$2.99	
☐ BAS50961-6	#19	Gargoyles Don't Drive School Buses	$2.99	
☐ BAS50962-4	#20	Wizards Don't Need Computers	$2.99	✓
☐ BAS22639-8	#21	Mummies Don't Coach Softball	$2.99	
☐ BAS84886-0	#22	Cyclops Doesn't Roller-Skate	$2.99	
☐ BAS84902-6	#23	Angels Don't Know Karate	$2.99	AC
☐ BAS84904-2	#24	Dragons Don't Cook Pizza	$2.99	
☐ BAS84905-0	#25	Bigfoot Doesn't Square Dance	$3.50	✓
☐ BAS84906-9	#26	Mermaids Don't Run Track	$3.50	
☐ BAS25701-3	#27	Bogeymen Don't Play Football	$3.50	
☐ BAS25707-3	#28	Unicorns Don't Give Sleigh Rides	$3.50	HC
☐ BAS25804-4	#29	Knights Don't Teach Piano	$3.50	✓
☐ BAS99552-9		Bailey School Kids Joke Book	$3.50	
☐ BAS88134-5		Bailey School Kids Super Special #1: Mrs. Jeepers Is Missing!	$4.99	
☐ BAS21243-5		Bailey School Kids Super Special #2: Mrs. Jeepers' Batty Vacation	$4.99	

Available wherever you buy books, or use this order form

- -

Scholastic Inc., P.O. Box 7502, Jefferson City, MO 65102

Please send me the books I have checked above. I am enclosing $_____ (please add $2.00 to cover shipping and handling). Send check or money order — no cash or C.O.D.s please.

Name _____

Address _____

City _____ State/Zip _____

Please allow four to six weeks for delivery. Offer good in the U.S. only. Sorry, mail orders are not available to residents of Canada. Prices subject to change.

BSK697